# FREDDY'S TEDDIES

*For Marie and Freddy, with love*

Scholastic Children's Books,
Commonwealth House, 1-19 New Oxford Street,
London WC1A 1NU, UK
a division of Scholastic Ltd
London ~ New York ~ Toronto ~ Sydney ~ Auckland

First published in the UK by Andersen Press Ltd, 1995
Published in Australia by Random House Australia Pty
This edition published by Scholastic Ltd, 1996

Copyright © Peter Melnyczuk, 1995

ISBN: 0 590 13881 2

Colour separated by Photolitho AG, Zurich, Switzerland
Printed in Hong Kong

All rights reserved

10 9 8 7 6 5 4 3 2

The right of Peter Melnyczuk to be identified as the author/illustrator of this
work has been asserted by him in accordance with the Copyright, Designs
and Patents Act, 1988.

# FREDDY'S TEDDIES

Written and illustrated by
Peter Melnyczuk

Freddy had three teddies, Pickles, Nick and Max. He loved them all, but his favourite was Max. Max was very old, so old that he had once belonged to Freddy's dad. Freddy loved the stories his dad told him about Max. They made him feel that Max was very special. Then, one day Freddy noticed something odd.

He woke one morning to find the three bears sitting in different parts of the room from where they had been the night before. Their faces were smeared with cream and their paws were sticky.

Freddy wondered how this could be. He decided to stay awake that night and find out.

Freddy waited and watched long into the night. He grew more and more sleepy. But just as he felt himself nodding off he heard the pit-a-pat of paws running across the floor. He sat up, his eyes open wide, and saw the three teddies tiptoeing out of the room.

Freddy put on his slippers and dressing gown and followed the three bears. Down the stairs and out of the house they went, down the garden path, out of the town, into the fields, through the meadows, along the stream and into a large wood.

"Where am I?" thought Freddy. The wood was very dark and, as he stumbled along, he wondered if he should have come this far. In the distance an owl hooted. For a moment Freddy was afraid that there might be lions or tigers in the wood, and he would never find his way home again. He couldn't see his teddies anywhere.

Just then Freddy stopped. He could hear the sound of music and happy laughter in the distance.

"It sounds like a party," he thought. He walked towards the noise, which grew louder. Through the trees he could see figures moving about. And then, in a clearing, he saw an amazing sight.

Hundreds of teddies were singing and dancing, jumping about and playing games in the moonlight.

Freddy stood and watched for a long time. He saw Pickles and Nick. But where was Max?

A breeze blew through the trees. Freddy shivered. Was that a voice softly calling his name? He looked up and there was Max.

"Hello, Freddy," he said, "I'm so glad you came. Now, come along with me!"

Max turned a somersault in the air and led Freddy through the trees.

Holding Freddy's hand, Max took him up, up, into the treetops, until they were looking down at the countryside stretched out far below. The villages and towns were still and quiet. But the woods and fields were alive with the animals of the night. Foxes raced across the meadows, badgers hunted for food, and owls swooped down from the trees to catch their prey.

"When the moon is full," said Max, "and people are fast asleep, we teddies come here to meet our friends.

"Only a few children are ever shown this place, Freddy. You must keep it a secret, or everybody will want to come and see and that will ruin it. But now, come and join our dancing and games."

Freddy danced and played until his eyes felt heavy.

"It's time you were in bed," said Max.

"Thank you for letting me join in," said Freddy, yawning.

Max caught hold of his hand and they flew through the air until Freddy saw his home far below. Max was smiling. "Goodnight, Freddy," he said.

"Goodnight, Max," said Freddy and he closed his eyes. He felt himself falling lightly through the air, falling, falling...

He woke with a start and sat up. It was daylight, and he was back home in bed; the bears were sitting on the floor.

Freddy felt disappointed. "It must have been a dream," he thought. He went downstairs.

"Dad," he said, "I've just had the strangest dream." Freddy started to explain about Max and the teddies' party.

"That wasn't a dream, Freddy," grinned his dad. "When I was young, Max took me to the teddy bears' party. Now he has taken you too and we must both take care to keep the teddies' precious secret."